ANCIENT GREEK MYTHS

PANDORA'S BOX

Author
Nick Saunders

Consultant
Dr Thorsten Opper, British Museum

First published in Great Britain in 2007 by ticktock Media Ltd.,
Unit 2, Orchard Business Centre, North Farm Road,
Tunbridge Wells, Kent, TN2 3XF

ticktock project editor: Jo Hanks
ticktock project designer: Graham Rich

We would like to thank: Indexing Specialists (UK) Ltd.

ISBN 978 1 84696 067 3
Printed in China
A CIP catalogue record for this book is available from the British Library.

CONTENTS

THE GREEKS, THEIR GODS & MYTHS

The ancient Greeks lived in a world dominated by the Mediterranean Sea, the snow-capped mountains that surrounded it, dangerous winds, and sudden storms. They saw their lives as controlled by the gods and spirits of Nature, and told myths about how the gods fought with each other and created the universe. It was a world of chance and luck, of magic and superstition, in which the endless myths made sense of a dangerous and unpredictable life.

The ancient Greek gods looked and acted like human beings. They fell in love, were jealous, vain, and argued with each other. Unlike humans, they were immortal. This meant they did not die, but lived forever. They also had superhuman strength and magical powers. Each god had a power that belonged only to them.

In the myths, the gods sometimes had children with humans. These children were born demi-gods and might have special powers, but were usually mortal and could die. When their human children were in trouble, the Olympian gods would help them.

The gods liked to meddle in to human life. Different gods took sides with different people. The gods also liked to play tricks on humans. They did this for all sorts of reasons: because it was fun; because they would gain something; and also for revenge. The Ancient Greeks believed that 12 Olympian gods ruled over the world at any time. The 10 gods and goddesses that you see here were always Olympians, they were the most important ones. Some of them you'll meet in our story.

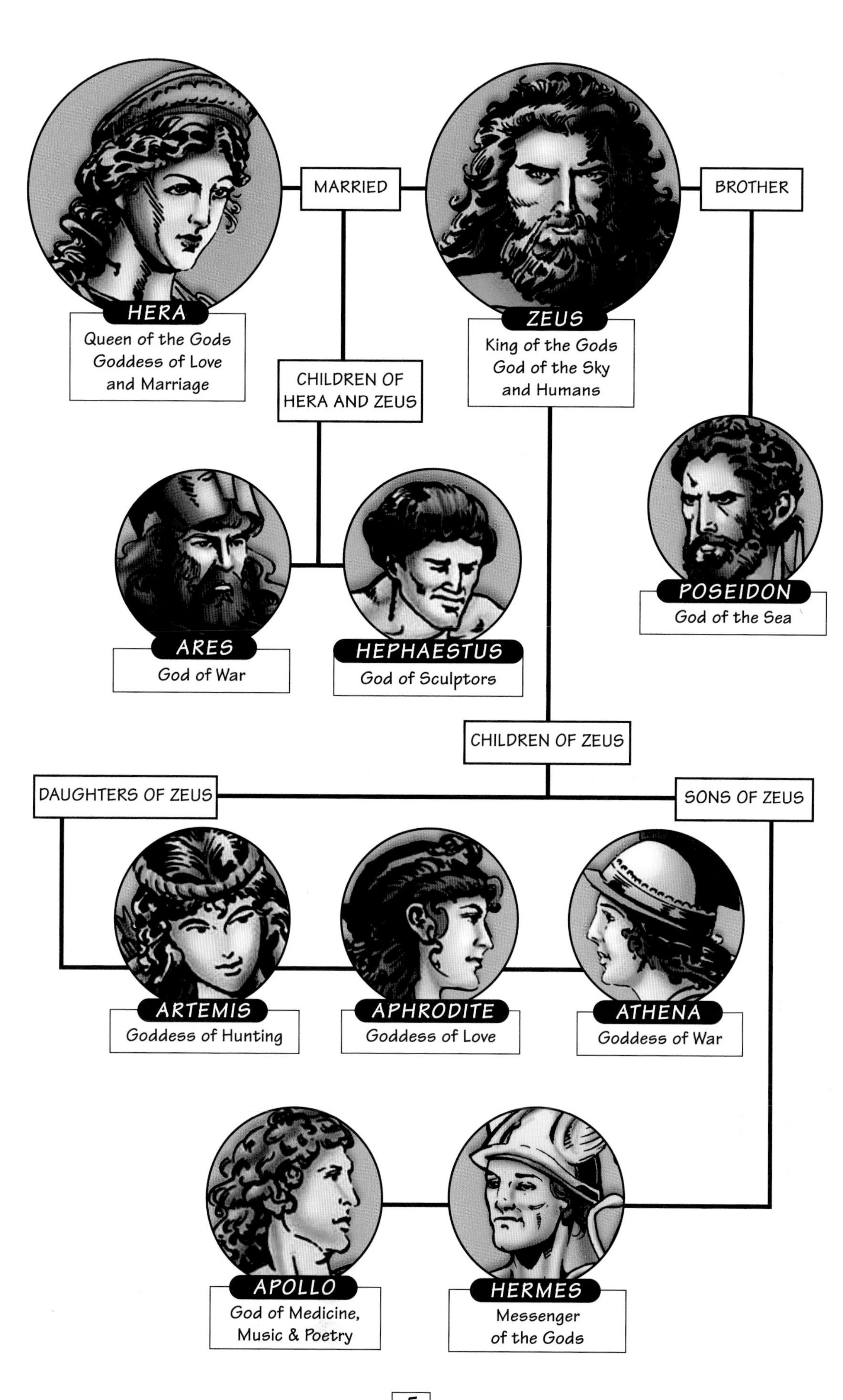
MARRIED
BROTHER
HERA
Queen of the Gods
Goddess of Love
and Marriage
ZEUS
King of the Gods
God of the Sky
and Humans
CHILDREN OF
HERA AND ZEUS
POSEIDON
God of the Sea
ARES
God of War
HEPHAESTUS
God of Sculptors
CHILDREN OF ZEUS
DAUGHTERS OF ZEUS
SONS OF ZEUS
ARTEMIS
Goddess of Hunting
APHRODITE
Goddess of Love
ATHENA
Goddess of War
APOLLO
God of Medicine,
Music & Poetry
HERMES
Messenger
of the Gods

SETTING THE SCENE

This story was used by the ancient Greeks to explain where men and women came from, and who created them. Before the Olympian gods ruled the heavens, there was another race of giant gods who were in charge. They were called the Titans. The Titans Prometheus, and his brother Epimetheus, created immortal men. When Prometheus stole the Olympian gods' fire for men, Zeus swore revenge. The ancient Greeks saw the strengths and weaknesses of men and women as beginning with the anger of Zeus. He created Pandora as the first woman and gave her a box full of evil spirits to bring suffering to all humankind, and to make them mortal. Life and death, happiness and tragedy, were inescapable parts of human nature, gifts from the gods.

Mount Olympus

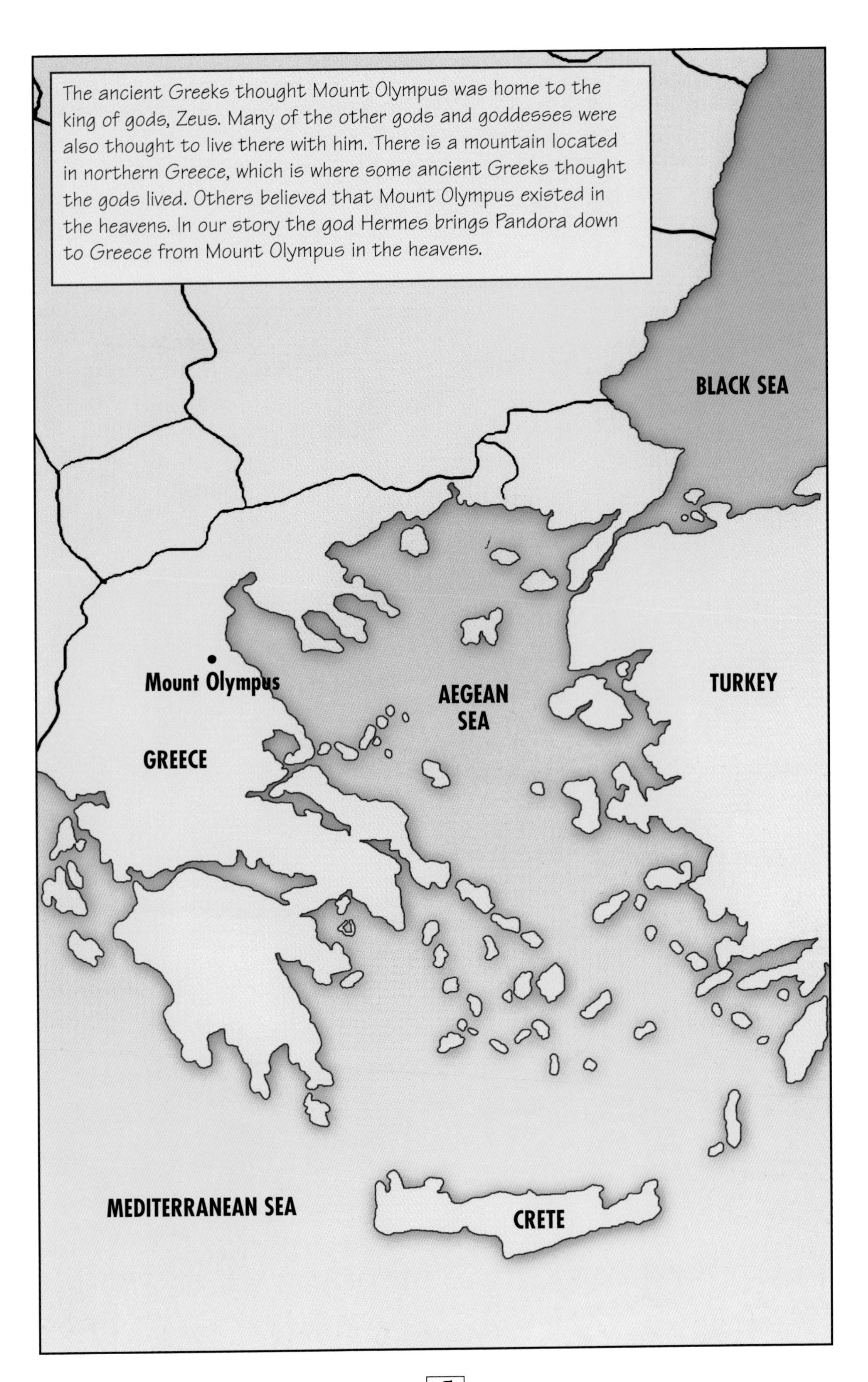
The ancient Greeks thought Mount Olympus was home to the king of gods, Zeus. Many of the other gods and goddesses were also thought to live there with him. There is a mountain located in northern Greece, which is where some ancient Greeks thought the gods lived. Others believed that Mount Olympus existed in the heavens. In our story the god Hermes brings Pandora down to Greece from Mount Olympus in the heavens.
BLACK SEA
Mount Olympus
AEGEAN SEA
TURKEY
GREECE
MEDITERRANEAN SEA
CRETE

A PERFECT LIFE

In the early times of gods and heroes, only men lived on Earth. They lived a life without pain, hunger, cold or illness. They also lived forever, like the gods. It was a time free from worries and troubles. These men were looked after by Prometheus, an old god, who took care of their every need… what more could these men want in their perfect life?

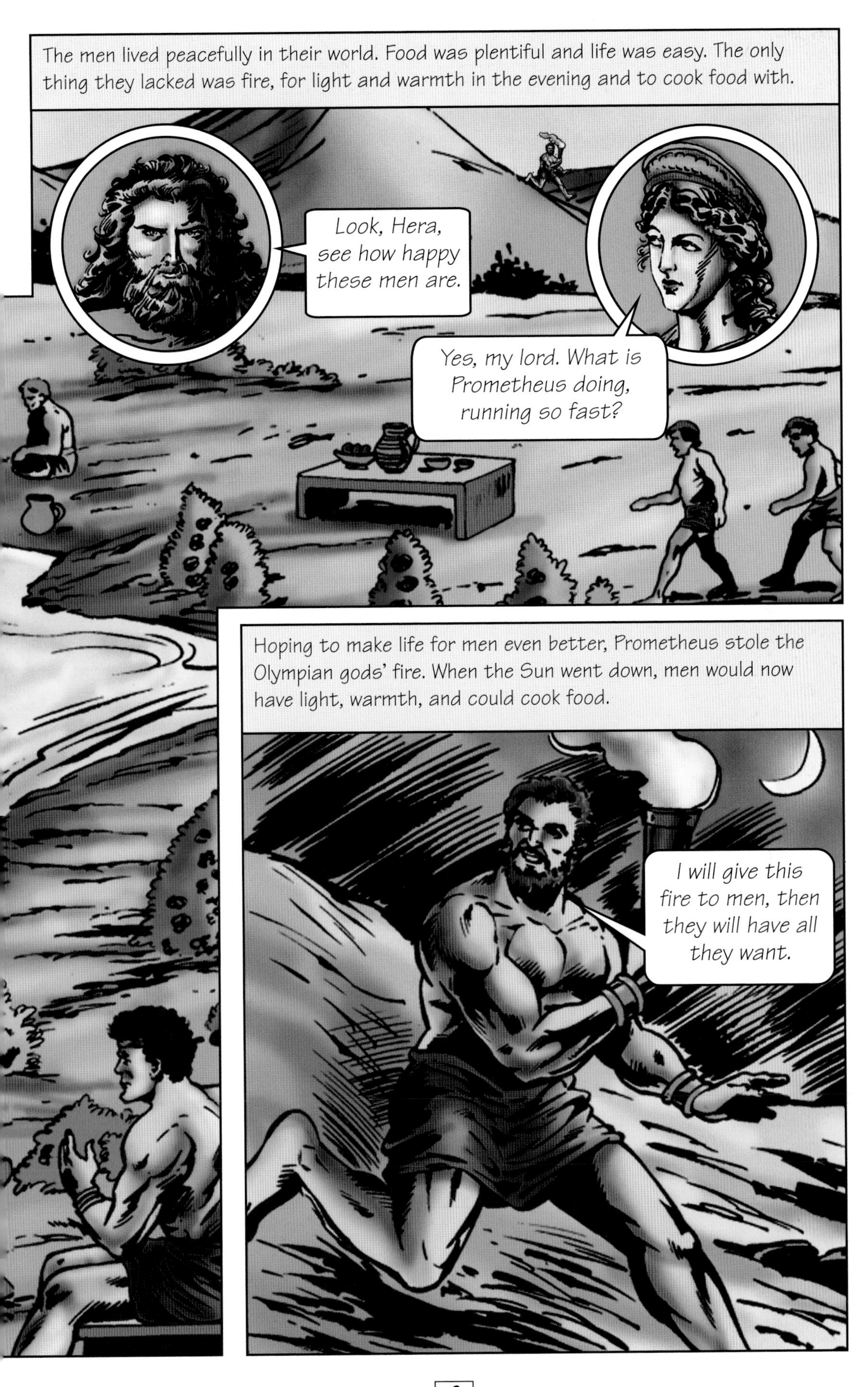
The men lived peacefully in their world. Food was plentiful and life was easy. The only thing they lacked was fire, for light and warmth in the evening and to cook food with.
Look, Hera, see how happy these men are.
Yes, my lord. What is Prometheus doing, running so fast?
Hoping to make life for men even better, Prometheus stole the Olympian gods' fire. When the Sun went down, men would now have light, warmth, and could cook food.
I will give this fire to men, then they will have all they want.

Zeus, king of the gods, was angry with Prometheus for stealing the god's prized fire. So he chained Prometheus to a mountain. Every day a monstrous vulture pecked at Prometheus' body. Every night Prometheus' wounds healed, but every day the vulture returned to make more.

One day, Zeus' son – the super-strong Hercules, heard Prometheus' screams. Always wanting to help people in pain, Hercules rushed to help him. He killed the vulture, and broke Prometheus' chains.

The news of Prometheus' escape angered Zeus. He wandered around his palace on Mount Olympus, thinking up another punishment for Prometheus.

THE FIRST WOMAN

Zeus decided to upset mankind to punish Prometheus. The punishment would be clever, and cruel. He would offer them a gift that appeared perfect on the outside, but once accepted would ruin their happy world. He needed the help of all the gods for his plan to work. First, he called on Hephaestus, god of sculptors, and ordered him to make a person from clay.

Zeus was overjoyed when Hephaestus showed him his sculpture. His creation was stunning. Now Zeus called his daughter, Athena, to bring her to life.

Now Zeus needed the other gods and goddesses to play their part in his clever plan. He called them to his palace, and asked each one to give his wonderful creation a gift.

Hermes was the messenger of the gods, and knew what men were like. He thought that this beautiful woman would have to be clever.
My gift will help you understand the thoughts of men.
Hermes, this is a most special gift. I know nothing of the ways of men.

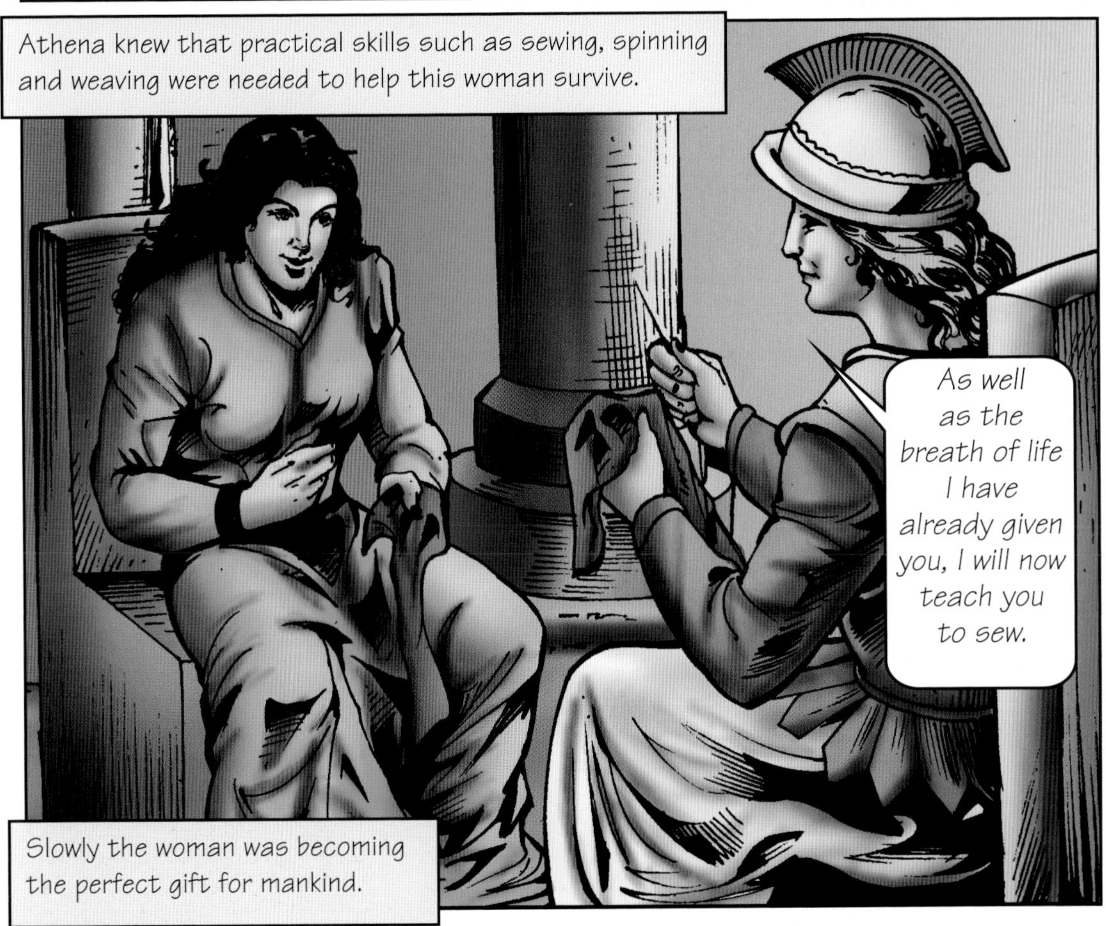
Athena knew that practical skills such as sewing, spinning and weaving were needed to help this woman survive.
As well as the breath of life I have already given you, I will now teach you to sew.
Slowly the woman was becoming the perfect gift for mankind.

Apollo was next. He was god of medicine, music and poetry. He gave the woman the ability to treat sickness and entertain.

Finally, it was Zeus' turn to give Pandora a gift.
What gift do you have for me, Zeus?
I ordered you to be created and now I will name you… Pandora, which means 'gifted with all.'
And I will also make you full of mischief and lazy.

Zeus ordered a great feast to be held on Mount Olympus. The gods and goddesses came to see Pandora, and each gave her a secret. Hephaestus, the sculptor, had created a magical box to hold these secrets. A glittering golden cord kept the box safely shut.

For every gift we gave you, Zeus asked us to put a special secret in this box for you. Be careful with it!
Pandora, take this box, but also remember this warning. Never open it, however much you want to.
Eat and be merry Olympian gods! We have obeyed our father Zeus, and made Pandora – the first woman for mankind.
Hera, Zeus' wife and queen of the gods, was the last to give Pandora her gift. By doing so, she made sure mankind would suffer…
From me you will have the gift of never-ending curiosity.

A NEW LIFE...

It was now time for Pandora to begin her new life on Earth. Hermes showed Pandora the way to Prometheus' home, taking her down the steep slopes of Mount Olympus to the world of men. How would she cope in this strange place, away from the gods? Would their gifts help her? And what of the secrets inside her magical box?

Pandora and Hermes did not receive a warm welcome. Prometheus was worried about Zeus' gift and wouldn't marry her. He told his brother, Epimetheus, also to ignore Pandora.

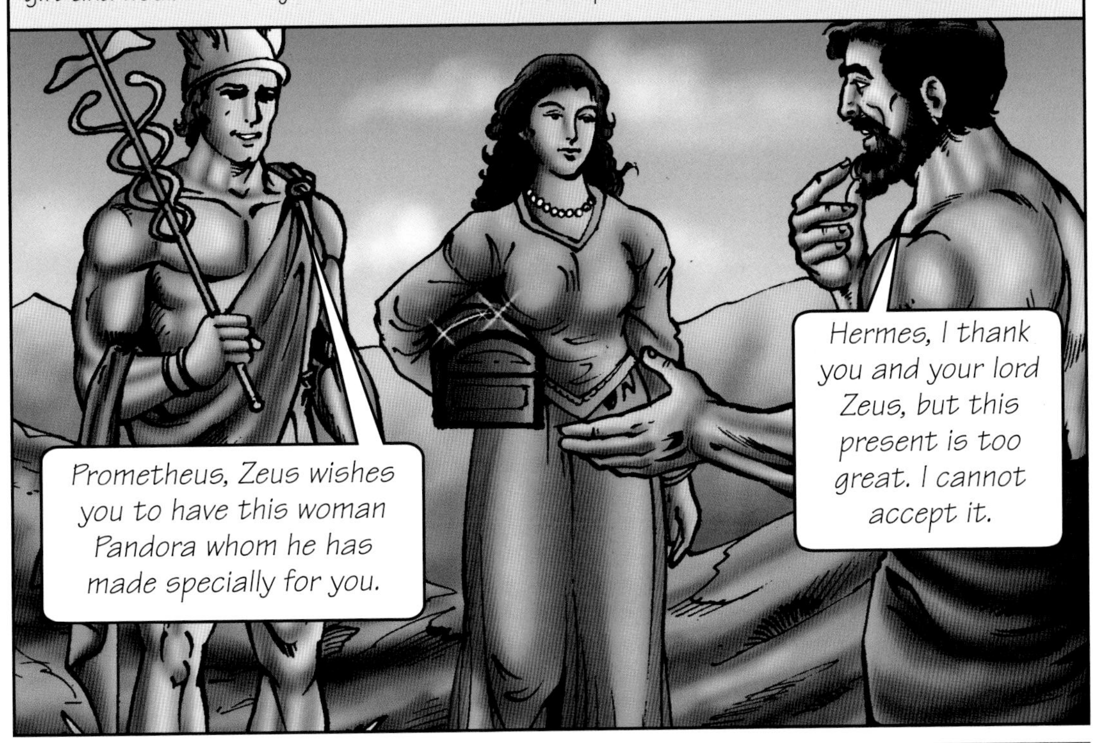

But Epimetheus was not as wise as his brother. The charms Aphrodite had given Pandora worked on him, and Epimetheus was fooled by her beauty.

Epimetheus fell deeply in love with Pandora. He was blinded by her charm and beauty, and soon they were married.

At first, Pandora and Epimetheus lived a wonderful life. They wanted nothing in their lives but each other's company.

The happy couple wandered Earth, hand in hand. They picked flowers, danced, played the lyre and ate sweet fruits. What could possibly make them unhappy?

Each day, Pandora polished her sparkling magical box. Despite Hera's gift of curiosity, Pandora had not opened it. But she really wanted to know what was inside.
Can Pandora resist her urge to open her box?
She cannot hold out for ever…
I haven't seen such a beautiful box anywhere. Surely it must keep safe some beautiful things, but I must remember Hephaestus' warning.

Each day, Pandora's curiosity grew and grew. She started to believe that she could hear voices in the box calling out to her.

Curiosity was starting to torture poor Pandora. She imagined that the box contained fabulous golden treasures and glittering jewels. If only she could look inside... just once!

As the days went by, Pandora imagined the voices in the box were getting louder. They shouted that she open the box to set them free.
You cannot ignore them much longer, Pandora!
Aarrgh! I can't stand it. The voices keep begging me to open the box. I must be strong though.
Pandora, set us free!

Pandora knew that she was weakening, and again remembered Hephaestus' stern warning. So she hid the box in an old cupboard. Surely, the voices would leave her alone now?

But, the voices got louder and louder. They called Pandora's name, trying to get her to open the box.
I will only hold it for a minute.
Open the box, Pandora.
Pandora, why won't you see us?
Pandora! Let us out to play.

Pandora knew she must fight the urge but felt unable to ignore the begging voices any longer. She put the box in a wooden chest and locked it shut with large iron chains.

LIFTING THE LID

Pandora and Epimetheus continued to live a happy life together, but secretly Pandora was troubled by the box. Although the voices no longer called constantly, they would still call. One night, the magic box filled her dreams and the voices cried out to her more loudly than ever. She woke up and crept to the garden, making sure that no-one saw her.

The boulder that had been hard to move over the chest, now magically jumped away. The chest lay in the hole where she had left it. The voices coming from it were deafening.

Pandora dug into the soil to lift out the wooden chest. She unlocked the chains then removed her magical box. She loosened the glittering cord that had held the lid tightly shut...

As soon as Pandora opened the box, a high-pitched whiny sound filled the air. She knew immediately that she had set free something terrible.
I knew your gift of curiosity would work, Hera!
Yes, lord Zeus, my gift to Pandora has finally set free your punishment.
I am Misery.
I am Grief.
I am Death.
I am Hunger.

Zeus had insisted that each god place a secret in Pandora's magical box. He ordered that it must be a nasty secret. Pandora now realised this and slammed shut the box's lid. But, it was too late.
Greed is my name.
Oh! By the power of Apollo, what have I done?
And I am Disease.
Horrible little winged creatures had flown out of the box. They buzzed round Pandora in a terrifying swarm. At last they were free on Earth…

The evils that escaped from the box started attacking. Never before had anyone on Earth felt such things. Anger and Misery were the first to strike.
What is happening? This is not right.
Epimetheus, I am so sorry. I opened the box and let loose all these terrible things!

Epimetheus felt anger for the first time. He shouted at his wife in a wild rage that frightened Pandora. What was wrong with her loving husband?

Epimetheus' angry shouting made Pandora cry. For the first time in her life she began to weep with sorrow, not joy.

Soon all the evils that Pandora had released from the box had swarmed to every corner of Earth. Everywhere they went men suffered, feeling miseries they never knew existed.

Anger, illness, disease, passion, greed, lies, jealousy, pain, crime, hunger, old age, death, sorrow and all the other curses found their way into every house and village, bringing despair to everyone.

Disease and old age struck every home. Everyone felt pain and suffering. There was no escape from the evils that Pandora had released.

Death and grief had also arrived, and with them came misery and hardship. Instead of living forever, everyone would now die. Soon, funeral pyres burned all over Earth.

IS THERE HOPE?

Epimetheus' anger grew as he realised the terrible pain Pandora had caused. For the first time, they fought. Now that evil and sorrow were everywhere, what hope was there for mankind? Even worse, Pandora could still hear a voice from her box... what further misery was hiding there?

Soon Epimetheus could also hear the voice. It was softer and sweeter than the others. Pandora and Epimetheus grew calm, as the voice grew louder. Together they decided that it was worth letting the creature out, if it could help. So, they carefully opened the box. A tiny winged creature flew out, it was quite different from the others.

Hope fluttered around Pandora and Epimetheus, touching them and making them feel better. They began to smile and be friends again.

After bringing happiness to Pandora and Epimetheus, Hope flew out of the window to help the rest of the world.

Hope brought happiness to everyone. Whatever evils they suffered, men could now look forward for a better future.

Pandora and Epimetheus now had Hope as a friend. Whenever things went wrong, hope would help them. Soon they had a baby daughter called Pyrrha, who brought them great happiness.
Epimetheus, see how beautiful our baby Pyrrha is!

When Pyrrha grew up she married Prometheus' son, Deucalion. Their world was happy. Even though it was filled with the evils from Pandora's box, Hope and the gods' fire made it better.
Yes, great Prometheus, thanks to you we are all now joined together in happiness.
At last! Hope and I have brought joy to Pandora's family and my own.

Zeus was still angry. Hera begged him to stop punishing Prometheus for stealing the fire. But Zeus ignored her and sent fierce storms to flood the world.

The only people to survive the floods were Pyrrha and Deucalion. With Hope at their side, they set about rebuilding the human race.

FULFILLING ZEUS' WISHES

The actions of Prometheus changed the world. People now faced misery and death. But Hope was always by their side. Was Zeus happy about what he had done?

Pandora had been the first woman on Earth. Through her daughter, Pyrrha, she was mother to all women. Wherever they lived, and whatever they looked like, they had her fine qualities... and endless curiosity!

Pandora's final gift of Hope remained in the hearts and minds of all men and women forever. Hope was always there to lift their spirits and help them through bad times.

GLOSSARY

Aphrodite: *Daughter of Zeus and Dione, and one of the twelve immortal Olympian gods. She was the goddess of love and passion and was married to Hephaestus.*

Apollo: *Son of Zeus and the Titaness Leto, and one of the twelve immortal Olympian gods. He was the god of prophecy and music, and worshipped especially at Delphi.*

Athena: *Daughter of Zeus, who was born fully grown and armed for battle from her father's forehead. One of the twelve immortal Olympian deities, she was the goddess of war and protector of cities.*

Banquet: *A large gathering of people feasting together. It was an important feature of ancient Greek society and it was believed that the Olympian gods also held banquets.*

Clay and water: *The two basic components used by Hephaestus to make Pandora. They represent the Earth, but needed Athena's heavenly breath to bring them to life.*

Curiosity: *The gift, or curse, given by Hera to Pandora. For the ancient Greeks, curiosity was a basic human instinct that could have a good or bad outcome.*

Deucalion: *Son of Prometheus, and husband of Pandora's daughter Pyrrha. Deucalion and Pyrrha were the only survivors of the great flood that Zeus sent to destroy the world.*

Dreams: *In ancient Greece, the gods spoke to mortals by appearing in dreams and visions, suggesting what they should do in particular circumstances.*

Fire: *Prometheus' gift to humankind which he stole from Olympus. Fire represented civilised life, providing warmth and light, and allowed food to be cooked, not eaten raw.*

Floods: *In Greek mythology, Zeus was also a weather god as well as King of Olympus. He used rain and flooding to punish mortals.*

Funeral pyre: *A specially built bonfire on which the dead were laid and then burned as part of traditional Greek funeral rites.*

Garlands: *In ancient Greece, flowers and leaves were woven together as decoration for the hair and body. They represented the beauty and fertility of nature in the world of humans.*

Gifts: *Greek gods often gave dangerous gifts to humankind. They could bring bad luck as well as good. Pandora's gifts brought misfortune despite being contained in a beautiful box.*

Hephaestus: *Son of Zeus and Hera, and one of the twelve immortal Olympian deities. He was the god of metalsmiths, craftsmen and* *sculptors. He built Zeus' palace and fashioned armour. He was also famous for being lame in one leg.*

Hercules: *Son of Zeus and the mortal woman Alcmena, and the most famous hero of Greek mythology. Tough and brave, Hercules freed Prometheus when Zeus chained him to a great rock.*

Hope: *The last winged-creature or spirit that Pandora released from her magic box. While all the other spirits brought misfortunes to humankind, Hope was able to conquer them all, and help people to live their lives.*

Lyre: *Stringed musical instrument common in ancient Greece. Lyre playing and music were among the gifts of Apollo to Pandora.*

Mount Olympus: *Traditionally regarded as the home of Zeus' immortal family of Olympian gods. Some thought it was a snow-capped mountain in northern Greece, others thought it was located in the Heavens.*

Oracles: *Temple-sanctuaries dedicated to the gods. By consulting them, the Greeks believed they could discover the will of the gods.*

Pearls: *Natural gems that form inside oyster shells. For the ancient Greeks they represented the beauty, fertility, and power of the sea. Poseidon gave Pandora a pearl necklace to protect her.*

Poseidon: *Son of Cronos and Rhea, elder brother of Zeus, and one of the twelve immortal Olympian deities. He was god of the sea.*

Pyrrha: *Daughter of Pandora and Epimetheus, she married Prometheus' son Deucalion. She and her husband were the only survivors of Zeus' great flood, and repopulated the earth.*

Titans: *A race of gods who ruled the world before Zeus and his Olympian deities. They were giant creatures, the offspring of Uranus (Sky) and Gaia (Earth).*

Voices: *In Greek mythology, the gods used mysterious voices to influence humans. Hera gave Pandora the gift or curse of curiosity. It took the form of voices that Pandora imagined were calling to her from inside the box.*

Vulture: *Large bird that lives on the flesh of dead animals. Zeus used it to punish Prometheus for stealing fire and giving it to humankind. In some versions of this myth the vulture is an eagle.*

Wind: *Zeus was a weather god as well as King of Olympus. Together with water, he used wind as his heavenly breath to bring destruction to the earth.*

INDEX